CLASSIC FAIRY TALES
The Golden Goose

Written by Barbara Hayes

Illustrated by Maurice Brownfoot

Library of Congress Cataloging in Publication Data

Hayes, Barbara, 1944-
  The golden goose.

  (Classic fairy tales) (Easy to read for little readers)
  Summary: A poor woodcutter's son is rewarded for his
kindness with the gift of a golden goose, which helps
him to win the hand of a princess.
  [1. Fairy tales.   2. Folklore—Germany]   I. Brownfoot,
Maurice, ill. II. Title. III. Series. IV. Series:
Easy to read for little readers.
PZ8.H325Go   1984   398.2'1'0943   [E]   84-17753
ISBN 0-86592-236-5

ROURKE ENTERPRISES, INC.
Vero Beach, Florida 32964

CLASSIC FAIRY TALES
The Golden Goose

Once upon a time there was a woodcutter. He and his family lived near a forest. He had three sons. The youngest was called Dummling. He was laughed at and made fun of by his family.

One day the eldest son went into the forest. He went to cut wood. His mother gave him an apple pie and a bottle of orangeade.

As he went into the woods, he met a little old man. The old

man said: "Please share your apple pie and orangeade with me."
The young man laughed. "Be off with you, old beggar," said he.

The young man started to cut down an elm tree. After a while he missed a stroke with the ax. He cut himself. He had to hobble home to bandage his cut. It was the little old man who had caused him to cut himself.

Next day, the second son set out to work in the forest. His mother gave him a big fruit cake and a bottle of lemonade. He too, met

the little old man. "Please share your cake and lemonade with me," said the old man.

The second son grinned. "Be off with you, old beggar," he laughed.

The young man started to cut down an oak tree. Suddenly, the ax slipped from his hand. The ax blade cut his leg. Like his brother, the day before, he limped home to bandage his leg. The old man had caused this to happen also. The day after,

Dummling said: "Father, now that my brothers cannot work, I will go and cut wood." His father replied: "No. You are too clumsy and stupid. Stay at home."

Dummling shook his head. "I really want to go," he replied.

"Then go, silly boy," said his father.

Dummling's mother gave him some stale bread and a bottle of water. He set off for the forest.

The little old man stopped him
as he reached the forest.
"Please give me something to
eat and drink," he said.
Dummling answered "I have only
stale bread and water. You are
welcome to that if it is good
enough for you."
The little man nodded.

They sat down. Dummling took out the stale bread. It changed into a juicy steak. Then he took out the bottle of water. It became a bottle of ginger ale. Dummling and the old man enjoyed their meal.

When they had
finished, the little
old man said:
"You have a kind
heart. You have
shared everything
with me. I will
make your fortune
for you."

He pointed to an old willow tree.
"Cut down that tree. You will
find something at the root."
Then he smiled, shook Dummling's
hand and went on his way.
It took Dummling several hours to
cut down the tree.

The tree fell at last.
Among the roots he found a goose
with feathers of real gold. He
gasped with astonishment.

He set off for home.
He was very tired
and hot.
He stopped
at an inn for a
cool drink.
The innkeeper had
three daughters.
When the
daughters
saw the
goose
they
were
very
curious.
They stared at the golden
bird. They all wished to
pluck one of its feathers.

At last the oldest
daughter said:
"I must have a
feather."
She waited till
Dummling had
turned his back.
Then she reached
out and pulled
off one of the tail
feathers of the goose.

To her surprise she found that
she could not free herself from
the feather. It stuck to her.

The second sister tried to free
her. The moment she touched her
sister she stuck to her as well.
The third sister put out her hand

to help the second sister. She
too, became stuck.
When Dummling finished his drink,

he set off for home again. He took
no notice of the three girls. As
he walked along, they had to
follow him.

The Town Mayor saw them.
"Foolish girls to run after a
young man like that," said he.
He grabbed the youngest girl's
hand to lead her away. The moment
he touched her, he too, got stuck
and had to follow.
The Mayor's assistant tried to
free him. He became stuck to the
Mayor. As the five went trudging
along, all stuck together, they
met two street cleaners.

The assistant called to the street
cleaners: "Please set us free."
As soon as they touched the
Mayor's assistant they, too, were
stuck. This made seven people
trotting after Dummling and his
golden goose. They came to a
city where a certain king reigned.

The King had an
only daughter.
She had never
laughed. "He who
can make my
daughter laugh
may marry her,"
the King had said.
The princess saw
Dummling and his
seven followers.
At once she burst
out laughing. "Just
look at those funny
people. They are

20

walking on
each other's
heels," she
laughed. The
moment she
laughed, all
seven people
were free. The
spell had been
broken. A few
weeks later,
Dummling and
the princess
were married.
They lived happily ever after.

Test your memory

Read the story first. Then try to answer these questions.

Who did the Mayor say was foolish? (Page 18).

Who became stuck to the Mayor? (Page 18).

What was the name of the youngest son? (Page 4)

Where did he find a goose? (Page 13).

After each question is the page number where you will find the answer.

To what did the old man point? (Page 12).

Whose hand did he shake? (Page 12).

What had the Princess never done? (Page 20).

What happened when she laughed? (Page 21).